Chime #2
Travelers

Advance praise for *The Sign of the Carved Cross*

"In *The Sign of the Carved Cross*, Lisa Hendey shows us what a modern girl and a saint from 1675 have in common. You'll find yourself relating to the characters, though you might be surprised by how. This isn't just a fun read: It's a chance to walk with a great saint."
—Sarah Reinhard, author and blogger, SnoringScholar.com

"Simply put, this is a beautiful story that leaves you wanting more. *The Sign of the Carved Cross*, the delightful second book in the popular Chime Travelers series, will leave young readers feeling confident after journeying through some powerful lessons that affect all school-aged kids today."
—Jennifer Willits, coauthor of *The Catholics Next Door: Adventures in Imperfect Living*

"From baptism to confession, catechesis to Church history, the smells of incense to the chime of the Church bells, Lisa Hendey uses the beautiful, everyday elements of the Catholic faith to bring the Chime Travelers stories to life. With engaging dialogue and scenes set to transport you back in time with Patrick and Katie, the fullness of Catholicism is taught in a way children can comprehend and are sure never to forget."
—Allison Gingras, blogger and radio host

"Imagine if you could travel back in time and meet the saints in person. Through the eyes of the Chime Travelers, Lisa Hendey helps us do just that! She brings them to life in a way that is fun and informative, while encouraging us to live their examples."
—Fr. Cory Sticha, Pastor, St. Mary's Parish, Malta, Montana

servant
AN IMPRINT OF
FRANCISCAN MEDIA
Cincinnati, Ohio

# The Sign of the Carved Cross

## LISA M. HENDEY
### ILLUSTRATED BY JENN BOWER

Cover and book design by Mark Sullivan
All illustrations by Jenn Bower

Library of Congress Control Number: 2015936959
ISBN 978-1-61636-848-7

Published by Servant Books,
an imprint of Franciscan Media
28 W. Liberty St.
Cincinnati, OH 45202
www.FranciscanMedia.org

Printed in the United States of America.
Printed on acid-free paper.
16 17 18 19  5 4 3 2

# ▲ Chapter One ▲

The recess bell announced the end to the day's math lesson at St. Anne's School. But you could barely hear it over the loud chimes of the old church bells next door. With bells ringing in the air, three girls hurried out the door of Mrs. Ray's classroom.

"Let's get out of here before she sees us," whispered Erin to her girlfriends Katie and Maria. They stepped out of the classroom into the sunshine. It was a warm May day, perfect for playing outside.

Two of the girls giggled. They were planning their escape from Lily—the new girl at St. Anne's—like it was a secret mission.

Katie didn't feel like laughing. She shot a glance in the direction of Lily and imagined how St. Anne's newest student must be feeling. But then again, Katie didn't want to make Erin mad. She ignored her guilty conscience and followed her friends.

Nearby, Katie's twin brother, Patrick, was gathering his buddies for a quick soccer match. Everyone at St. Anne's knew the twins. Katie was taller and Patrick was sportier. Both were smart, with bright red hair and tons of freckles. They both loved wearing jeans and hoodies. And the twins were so close that sometimes it seemed like they could read each other's minds.

But the Brady twins were acting funny lately. For the past few weeks, Patrick seemed to be in a lot less trouble than usual. And Katie, usually the nicest girl in class, was just a little less nice. Nobody was sure what was up.

So Katie and Maria followed Erin out the door to their favorite spot next to the field. They completely ignored Lily as they passed her. Katie tried to ignore the expression on Lily's face.

Outside, Katie and the girls stood in a trio, watching Patrick, Pedro, and Gregory run around the field.

"They say she doesn't have a dad," whispered Erin. "What's up with that?"

"Maybe that's why she looks so funny," Katie grumbled.

"Funny?" Maria said. "I think she's beautiful! That hair—and she has awesome shoes! I bet she has tons of cool clothes too. I mean, she could *totally* be a model when she grows up...or even now, if she tried!"

"Well, who knows *what* she'll try?" Erin answered. "I can't believe they even let her in to St. Anne's. She probably won't be around long."

Thinking jealously about Lily's pretty hair and cool shoes, Katie, too, hoped Lily would be gone soon.

# ▲ Chapter Two ▲

*Bbrriiinnngggg....*

As the recess bell chimed calling them back to class, Katie felt a bit guilty about saying something so mean about Lily. But there was another feeling going on too, one she couldn't quite name.

All the other girls at St. Anne's suddenly seemed so grown up. Katie wanted to be one of the popular girls. But she wasn't sure about the stuff she was starting to hear them say. She didn't really care about how her hair looked or what clothes she was wearing. What would they think if they knew she still slept with a stuffed animal? *They'd probably call her a baby...*

Cc Dd Ee
Ff Gg Hh
Prime Numbers!
· greater than 1
· can only be ÷
by 1 and itself
2, 3, 5, 7, 11, 13, 17
19, 23, 29, 31, 37, 41
Homework Assi
A–C
D–F
G–J
K–P
V–Z
DOGOODERS VI.
ENGLISH
GOD IS IN THE MATH
MRS. KAY
SILENCE IS GOLDEN

Katie promised herself that she would talk to Patrick about Lily after school. She headed back to her desk in the front row of the classroom. Her twin scooted into the desk next to her. His red hair was a mess and his white uniform shirt was covered with grass stains.

"You smell like a soccer ball," Katie whispered, giggling. She knew Patrick wouldn't have time to tease her back. But even if he did have the time, Katie doubted that Patrick would say anything mean to her. Something had happened to him in the past few weeks. He had changed.

He was even being extra nice to Gregory, the class saint. In the past, Gregory had always been the target of Patrick's teasing. But now Patrick was being very kind to the boy everyone else went out of his or her way to harass. Something was definitely up!

Just a few weeks ago, Patrick was taking his silly frog Francis to their adopted baby sister Hoa Hong's baptism ceremony. The next thing Katie

knew it was like he had a brand-new personality!

Mom and Dad had been so mad at Patrick when Francis had accidentally jumped into the baptismal font on Hoa Hong's big day that they'd made the entire Brady family volunteer for the St. Anne's "Cleaning Team." And after only a few weeks of Saturday cleanings, it seemed to Katie that Cleaning Team had already taught her twin a thing or two. On the other hand, being in the church so much had made Katie surprisingly unhappy. Before, Katie had been the twin most eager to go to church. Now Patrick was the one who wanted to go. Katie was a little envious of his renewed faith.

Patrick still insisted to Katie that something sort of crazy had happened to him a few weeks ago at Saint Anne's Church. And Katie honestly wasn't sure whether she really believed any of his story. *It all seemed too impossible...*

...those old, very, very loud church bells chiming...

...the floor suddenly rumbling...

...a strong wind blowing...

...and Patrick magically transported to Ireland? And meeting St. Patrick?

*Right! Sure that had happened!* Katie thought, still doubting Patrick's incredible story.

Katie had decided to keep Patrick's secret between the two of them, like he'd asked. But she was afraid her brother had gone a bit nuts. She did have to admit, though, that he'd been weirdly different ever since.

*Oh well, it was probably just what Mom would call "a phase." He'll probably be back to his normal, goofy self soon,* Katie thought to herself.

She glanced at her brother, who was paying attention to Mrs. Ray and not goofing off with Pedro like he used to do. Then again, maybe he really *had* changed after all.

# ▲ Chapter Three ▲

"Quiet down, kids," Mrs. Ray called from the front of the noisy classroom. "Before we get started with our Religion lesson, I wanted to take some time for all of us to get to know our new classmate better. Lily, could you come up here for a minute with me?"

Half the class, including Maria and Erin, laughed nervously at Lily as she walked to the front.

"Welcome, Lily," Mrs. Ray said as the tall new student walked forward. Lily's dark, shiny hair swayed as she moved. "I'm sorry we didn't have time to do this first thing this morning, but we'd love to know more about you and your family and what brought you to St. Anne's!"

The giggles continued as if everyone could sense how nervous Lily felt.

"There's not too much to tell," Lily shared quietly, her dark eyes focused on the floor. "It's just me and my mom really. We moved here to be closer to my grandparents. We've actually move around a lot the last few years since..." She stopped herself without explaining why. "My mom has a new job," Lily continued, "And she thought it would be nice if I could spend more time with my Nana and Gramps."

"So, do you have any hobbies?" Mrs. Ray prompted Lily, trying to help the new girl open up. "Do you play any sports?"

The question brought the first smile of the day to Lily's face. "I love to ride horses," she shared.

Cc Dd Ee
Ff Gg Hh
Genesis
Exodus
Leviticus
Bible
Bingo
OLD TESTAMENT
NEW TESTAMENT
BUTLER'S
Lives of the Saints
SILENCE IS
GOLDEN
K-P
U-Z
ME

"And now that I'm here, my mom says I can start weekly lessons!"

"That's great, Lily," Mrs. Ray encouraged. "You and Katie will have a lot in common, won't you, Katie? Lily, Katie has been riding for years! I bet you'll both take lessons at the same stables."

With that, the entire class looked towards Katie, who was staring at Mrs. Ray in surprise and horror. The last thing she wanted to do was babysit Lily!

"We'll see, Mrs. Ray," she answered, using one of her mom's favorite phrases. Katie was old enough to know that it definitely *didn't* mean, "Yes, sure! I would love to take care of this new girl!" Part of her thought Lily seemed nice. But what would Erin and Maria say?

*"We'll see..."*

# ▲ Chapter Four ▲

"*Katie, Patrick*, can you two come down here, please?" Mom called from the living room. It wasn't really a question. The twins knew from the sound of Mom's voice that she was feeling stressed out. So they dropped their Masterblaster controllers and raced down the stairs.

"What's up, Mom?" Patrick asked cheerfully. Katie stood nearby, rolling her eyes. She loved helping with their adopted baby sister. But in the past few weeks, Patrick was the one who was excited to help with Hoa Hong. The nicer Patrick became, the crankier Katie felt.

"I really need ten minutes to grab a shower, guys," Mom sighed. "Now that Hoa Hong is crawling, she's into everything! Could you two possibly take her out for a short walk?"

"Sure thing!" the twins said, laughing when they answered exactly the same way. Laughing made Katie's bad mood melt away a little.

"Let's go, little Rosebud," she cooed to her sister. She loved the way Mom and Dad had kept Hoa Hong's Vietnamese name but also nicknamed her in honor of their family's favorite saint, St. Thérèse, the "Little Flower."

"She sure doesn't smell like a rosebud," Patrick groaned as he lifted Hoa Hong into her stroller.

Katie laughed. "We'll let Mom deal with that when we get back from the walk!"

Katie took charge of pushing Hoa Hong's stroller down the street, while Patrick walked next to her, dribbling his soccer ball. When he got too far ahead, he would stop and practice juggling the ball off his knees until Katie caught up.

Patrick was always a bundle of energy. That's why Katie was surprised when he stopped at a certain point along their walk and looked straight at her.

"Hey," he asked. "What's up with you and that new girl? What's her name, Leah?"

"You mean, *Lily*?" Katie replied, her voice suddenly dropping a notch. Patrick noted a shift in his sister's tone.

"Yeah, *Lily*..." Patrick responded. "What's up with her? I mean, she seems pretty cool. Are you going to start hanging out with her?"

"What do you care?" Her mood changed as suddenly as a thunderstorm. "Why? *Do you like her or something*?"

Katie knew teasing her brother about a girl was a sure way to shut him up. And she definitely wanted to shut Patrick up, because the last thing she felt like talking about was the new girl.

"*No way!*" Patrick responded. "It's just that..." he hesitated.

"Just what?" Katie snarled. "Just that she's the tallest girl in class? That she has the most beautiful hair? Or that she loves horses and that she's probably an amazing rider?"

"I see," Patrick smiled at Katie. "*You're jealous. That's why you're acting so weird!*"

"Weird?" Katie answered, a little too fast. "What's weird is some new girl showing up with no dad. Why should I be jealous of some girl who just lands out of nowhere? Why should I even bother to get to know her? She'll probably be gone before anyone even learns her name."

Patrick looked at Katie, surprised by her sudden meanness.

"Well, maybe we should give her a chance, Katie," Patrick suggested. "It's sad that she's such a loner. Have you seen her at recess? She just sits on the swing all by herself..."

"Is that my fault?" Katie asked, sounding mad.

"Am I supposed to drop all of my friends and go hang out with her?"

"But Katie," Patrick said, stopping and looking his twin in the eye. "You're usually everyone's best friend! You're nice to everyone... *except Lily...*"

Katie felt tears in her green eyes. She knew she was being mean to Lily. She knew Lily was lonely. She just couldn't figure out what to do about it. If she tried being nice to Lily, Erin would stop talking to her. And everyone loved Erin. So if Erin was mad at Katie, everyone else would be, too.

And Katie knew she didn't want to be the lonely one...so she'd just ignore Lily for now.

"Come on," Katie said without really giving Patrick an answer. "Let's just get back to the house. I don't want to be late for riding lessons."

# ▲ Chapter Five ▲

By the time they pulled up at the stables an hour later, Katie was feeling a bit better. She jumped out of Mom's red van, grabbing her pink backpack. Lots of the girls at St. Anne's had that same backpack. But Katie could always tell hers because of "Rosie," a little clip-on stuffed horse that was stuck on the top of her pack. Rosie was Katie's good luck charm.

Wherever Katie went, she always had her pack and Rosie, too. She'd had Rosie on her backpack since kindergarten. That was long before the Brady family had adopted Hoa Hong. Katie knew that pretty soon she'd have to take Rosie off her pack if she didn't want to look like a baby, but she wasn't quite ready to do it yet.

"Here I am, Belle," Katie called to a beautiful brown horse. "Ready for a ride, girl?"

Katie looked forward to Friday all week long! Patrick was off at soccer practice, school was done for the week, and it was time for her weekly riding lesson at Reinhard's Stables. She'd been riding for almost five years now, so she was one of the more experienced riders. But every week with Belle felt like a new adventure.

*Clang, clang, clang.*

*Clang, clang, clang.*

In the distance, Katie heard Miss Elizabeth, her riding instructor, ringing the giant triangle. That meant that it was time to get down to business. Miss Elizabeth was a college student. She had been riding since she was Katie's age. Katie wanted to be just like her when she grew up.

Moving quickly, Katie organized Belle's tack. She already had her own helmet and boots on, so now it was time to get Belle ready for the ride. There were more than fifty horses at Reinhard's, but Belle had always been Katie's favorite. Something about their personalities really clicked.

Katie brushed Belle and was busily tacking up the horse when she heard Miss Elizabeth walk up behind her.

"Hey, Katie, how's it going?"

the young woman called out in her usual friendly voice.

"It's great, Miss..." Katie started to reply brightly before turning to see that her riding coach was not alone.

"I think you already know Lily, don't you, Katie?" Miss Elizabeth asked.

"Um, sure..." Katie responded. Her good mood started to slip away. "We go to St. Anne's together. How's it going, Lily?"

Katie was pretty sure that Lily recognized her lack of friendliness.

"I'm awesome, Katie," Lily replied, her smile a little forced. "I'm so excited about my first lesson. And it's so nice of you to help me get Belle ready."

"Help you—?" Katie started.

"Yes," Miss Elizabeth interrupted. "With this being Lily's first time and all, and you being such an experienced rider, I just knew that you'd love to share Belle today and help Lily with her first lesson. You'll be riding Peerybingle today."

Katie's heart fell. Peerybingle, the most mischievous horse at Reinhard's, was nobody's favorite. He was the most likely to kick you or throw you. He had a mind of his own.

"Lucky you, Belle," Katie grumbled under her breath a few minutes later as she watched Lily climb the mounting block and prepare to mount the horse Katie had long considered to be her own. She couldn't help but notice how graceful Lily looked in the saddle. "You get to hang out with Lily today. You'll probably forget all about me now."

# ▲ Chapter Six ▲

The next day, the Bradys' van pulled into St. Anne's parking lot fifteen minutes before noon. They were actually early for once!

Katie remembered how their family's Saturday Cleaning Team volunteer job had really started as sort of a punishment for something Patrick had done. But now, after only a few weeks, Mom and Dad and the twins were realizing how much more like home their parish felt.

The twins were happy to run into Father Miguel on their way into the narthex. "Hey, Father!" both called out in unison. Their voices bounced off the high ceilings in the entryway to the main church.

"Well, if it isn't the Brady Bunch," the young priest responded, as if that old joke never stopped being funny. "Mrs. Danks has your jobs all lined up for today."

"Katie," Mrs. Danks added with her sweet Irish accent, "Father Miguel and I want you to spend some time dusting in the Adoration Chapel today if that's OK with you."

"Sure, Mrs. Danks," Katie replied.

"I could help her, Father," Patrick offered.

"Thanks, Patrick," Father Miguel said. "But this is a mission for Katie."

Katie picked up her pink backpack and threw it over one shoulder. She turned to walk through the glass doors that separated the chapel from the main church, Rosie swinging from her strap.

"Oh, hey, Katie," someone whispered as Katie entered the Adoration Chapel. "I didn't know you come to Cleaning Team!"

Katie looked over the tops of the pews in the dimly lit space to see Lily cleaning the pews near the back of the chapel. Her heart sank.

"Yeah, my mom makes us come," Katie said in a low voice. "Like we don't have anything better to do on a Saturday than clean the stupid church..." It wasn't exactly how she felt, but Katie shrugged away her guilt.

"Oh, I don't know," Lily responded, somehow matching Katie's bad attitude with a sunny answer. "Maybe it's just because I'm new, but this seems like a pretty great way to help out at St. Anne's. Father Miguel invited me to come— probably because he knew my mom works on Saturdays and I'd be stuck watching game shows all day with Nana and Gramps if I stayed home!"

The new girl's laugh bounced off the stone walls and marble floor of the chapel. Katie felt her heart begin to soften a bit. She thought of Erin and frowned. Katie wasn't ready to line up for the job of President of the Lily Fan Club!

"So you live with your grandparents, huh? Where's your dad?" she asked. The laughter that had brightened Lily's face vanished. Katie knew she was being mean, but she couldn't help herself.

"Um, it's *complicated*," was the only answer Lily gave. "I've got to go vacuum the altar rug now. I guess I'll see you later."

Katie missed the single tear that ran down Lily's cheek as she rushed out of the small prayer space. For a second, Katie felt the satisfaction of seeing her words affect Lily.

But the moment Lily stepped out of the chapel, Katie felt horrible. Why was she acting like this when Lily was trying so hard to be friends? She sighed and knew she needed to talk to God. Maybe talking to him would help her figure out what was going on inside of her. As Katie knelt, she felt a prayer begin to form in her heart.

*"I'm not sure what's wrong with me, God,"* Katie whispered, praying out loud in the silent chapel.

Katie's quiet prayers were cut short by the first chime of St. Anne's loud bells. They rang nine times at noon each day as a reminder to pray the midday Angelus prayer. They'd been ringing that way for years, so loudly that everyone could hear them, even miles away.

*Clang, clang, clang...*

"I don't understand why I'm being so mean," Katie continued praying as the bells chimed three more times. "Everything feels so hard sometimes. I just want to be like Erin...everybody loves her! But I'm not. I'm not pretty at all..."

Three more chimes rang, and Katie suddenly felt the floor of the church begin to rumble and rock.

With the last three chimes, the glass door of the chapel blew open in a strong rush of cold wind.

And suddenly, everything became a blur.

# ▲ Chapter Seven ▲

Katie screamed and covered her head, unsure what was happening. An instant later, the chiming and rumbling stopped. Everything was silent, until Katie heard an odd crackling sound.

Katie smelled fire. Her knees were pressed into something hard. She was afraid to open her eyes. But that smoky smell seemed to be growing stronger. Reluctantly she peeked through her lashes, and was shocked at what she saw. Her knees weren't pressed against the smooth chapel floor anymore! She was kneeling on dirty, rocky ground.

She wasn't in the chapel at all! Instead she was in a long wooden cabin. Around her, the walls were made of tall wooden poles and covered in bark. A small campfire burned nearby, warming a clay pot.

Strangely, her backpack was on the ground next to her. She stood and pulled Rosie off the strap of her pack. She began to feel panic rising inside. She moved toward the end of the structure. As she walked, she passed woven mats and simple wooden furniture.

Animal skins were hanging from the ceiling. They divided the cabin into small sleeping areas. Long rows of simple beds lined the walls. Dried plants and vegetables tied in bunches hung from the roof.

"Where are we, Rosie?" Katie whispered to the small stuffed horse. She didn't care how silly it seemed to talk to a stuffed animal. She was trying hard not to cry!

"*Kwehkwe,*" Katie heard a quiet voice behind her say from the shadows. "You are welcome here, friend."

Katie spun around. At first, she didn't see anything. But when her eyes had adjusted to the dimly lit room, Katie could see a girl.

The girl's face was partially hidden by a red blanket. She wore a simple cotton blouse. Her skirt was made of some type of animal skin. Her leggings and shoes looked almost like the moccasins Erin liked to wear on free dress days. The girl's long black hair was swept into neat braids. Around her shoulders, pulled almost over her head, was that deep red blanket.

Katie resisted the urge to scream. Instead, she tried to remember her manners. "Thank you," she answered. But her voice was shaking from fear. "Where am I? Is Father Miguel here?"

Katie realized the girl was looking at her jeans, her tennis shoes, and especially at Rosie and her pink backpack with some confusion.

"Father Miguel?" the girl asked. "This is not a familiar name to me. Is he one of the new Blackrobes?"

"Father Miguel is the priest at St. Anne's. I was just cleaning the chapel. I closed my eyes for a minute to pray... the bells started chiming...and now I'm here."

Suddenly she thought of Patrick and everything he had said happened to him. "I need to find my brother."

# ▲ Chapter Eight ▲

Katie looked around, desperate to find a way out. She felt a light hand on her shoulder. When she turned, she was face-to-face with the girl, who was only a few inches taller than her. Up close, she looked much older.

"Welcome to our longhouse," the stranger said in an interesting accent. "I am Tekakwitha. This is my uncle's home, and my home too. I am going into the woods to collect firewood and water. Will you come with me?"

"The woods?" Katie responded, laughing nervously. But then she looked at Tekakwitha and what she saw stopped her giggles.

The girl was short, but she was clearly a teenager. What struck Katie most was Tekakwitha's face. It was covered with scars. Tekakwitha wore the blanket loosely over her long black hair. She pulled the blanket down to shield her eyes. Katie had never seen such dark eyes before.

"Uh, no, thank you," Katie responded, again walking toward the door. "I'd better get back to the chapel."

"Do not be afraid," Tekakwitha said kindly, again placing her hand on Katie's shoulder. "The marks you see on my face will not harm you."

Katie was embarrassed. "Oh, I wasn't trying to say..." Katie stuttered, stepping backwards.

"These are the marks of a terrible illness. The sickness spread through my people many years ago. Now I live with my uncle and his wife. Their daughters are now my sisters. This longhouse is our home."

Katie again looked around her at the large wooden building. It looked like it could hold almost a hundred family members.

"Wow, you must have a big family!"

The thought reminded her of her brother. She still had no idea where she was. But her mind flashed to Patrick and his story of Ireland. And to those loud bells chiming at St. Anne's...

"I was born to my mother and father eighteen years ago," Tekakwitha explained. "He was Iroquois, a great Mohawk chief. My mother was an Algonquin. My father's clan captured my mother. They took her away from her family to live with them. My father saw how beautiful she was, both inside and out. They were married and soon began a happy family. I came first, then my younger brother."

"But where are they now?" Katie asked.

"The great sickness came to our longhouse—they called it smallpox. It spread quickly, killing many in my tribe. The smallpox killed my parents and my baby brother. I am the only one in my family who survived. It left me with these marks across my face. My eyes can barely see. Many of those who live in this village laugh at me. They call me "she who bumps into things." Now, I live with my Uncle Iowerano. He became the next chief after my father died."

"A chief's daughter!" Katie responded. "You must be really popular around here."

"I am not," Tekakwitha said, a sad smile crossing her face. "In fact, I am hated."

Katie couldn't imagine how anyone could hate this sweet, quiet young woman. For a moment, Katie was so caught up in Tekakwitha's story that she forgot she was stuck in the middle of nowhere.

"But why?" Katie asked.

"I am different," Tekakwitha simply stated. "It is not what is on the outside that separates me from my people," Tekakwitha replied, her eyes shining. "You see, my mother was a Christian woman before she ever met my father and came to live in his home. She knew the one true God. My people—and especially my uncle—do not like the Blackrobes or the Christian faith they teach."

"Who are the Blackrobes?" Katie asked.

"They bring us the Good News of the Gospels," Tekakwitha explained. "They teach us about the One True God, about his son Jesus and his Church. The Blackrobes take care of sick people. And they pour special water over the heads of those who want to know Jesus and his Church."

"Oh, you mean priests!" Katie said excitedly.

"Where are these priests? You need to take me to them right away! They can probably help me find Father Miguel."

"I do not know this Father Miguel you speak of. But we do have a Blackrobe, Father de Lamberville, who is new in this place. I have recently begun to speak with him, to learn from him," Tekakwitha whispered, looking around the longhouse. She seemed to be very afraid, though Katie couldn't understand why.

"Come with me," Tekakwitha said. She pulled the red blanket over her head and walked towards the door of the longhouse. "I will take you to the chapel."

"Great!" Katie felt relief and hope. "Let's get going!"

# ▲ Chapter Nine ▲

Together, Tekakwitha and Katie walked the wooded path between the longhouse and the chapel. Katie's mind was going in a million different directions at once.

*"Where am I?"* she asked herself. *"How did I get here? And how am I ever going to find my way home? Dad and Patrick must be freaking out by now. They've probably even called Mom to see if she knows where I am. Hopefully this Blackrobe we are going to see will know how to get me back to St. Anne's. I mean, he's a priest, right? Surely he'll know Father Miguel..."*

Then Katie's mind flashed to her twin. He had told Katie about his trip to Ireland. Patrick insisted that he had magically traveled in time. He even said that he'd met St. Patrick!

"How could it be, Rosie?" Katie whispered to the little stuffed horse. She hoped Tekakwitha wouldn't hear her. She was so confused! As they walked, their shoes crunched the leaves that covered the path. Katie tried to figure out where—and *when*—she could possibly be.

Next to Katie, Tekakwitha walked along the path with a slight limp. One of her legs was hurting. She used the blanket over her head to keep the sunlight out of her face and eyes.

"Are you OK?" Katie asked with concern. "You're limping."

"I am nearly healed; *nia:wen*, thank you," Tekakwitha said, smiling. "This injury has actually changed my life. So I give thanks to God for it. Along with it came great blessings."

"A hurt foot changed your life?" Katie asked. She couldn't imagine any good that could come from an injury like that. One time she'd fallen and hurt her arm while riding Belle. When that happened, she had to take a break from riding at Reinhard's Stables for two whole months.

"Yes," Tekakwitha continued. "You see, I was gathering wood with the women of my longhouse one day. I fell and injured myself. A few days later, I was alone in the longhouse. I was hurt too badly to work outdoors that day, so I stayed inside. I saw a shadow pass by the doorway. It was the new Blackrobe, Father de Lamberville."

"Did you invite him to come in?" Katie asked. If Father Miguel stopped by to visit Dad, her own family usually dropped everything to welcome him. *Of course that suspiciously seemed to always happen around dinnertime*, Katie thought to herself with a smile.

"I did. I believe that God sent Father de Lamberville to me that day," Tekakwitha said with a shy smile. "You see, for so many years I had longed to know more of the Christian ways. I remembered my mother, in my childhood, quietly sharing her prayers and stories with me."

Katie thought of her own mother, who had always prayed with her when she was little.

"In recent years," Tekakwitha continued, "many Mohawks have come to know Jesus Christ. The Blackrobes teach us with paintings, with games and with stories. We even have the new chapel now, St. Peter's. It is a longhouse built especially for prayer and holy Mass."

"But why did you have to wait for God to send the priest to you Tekakwitha?" Katie asked curiously. "Couldn't you just go to church like everyone else?"

"Oh no," Tekakwitha explained, her eyes cast downward. "You see, although my mother was a Christian, my uncle—the chief—still hates the Blackrobes. He was already very angry with me. He wanted me to marry a young man, but I refused."

"But that's not fair," Katie responded. "They can't tell you who to marry!"

"We Mohawks marry to support our families," Tekakwitha explained. "The new husband moves into the home of his bride. He becomes her husband. But he is also a helpful member of her family. He is a hunter, a protector, and a caretaker."

Katie looked at Tekakwitha's sad face. This was a hard story for her to tell. Katie decided not to push her. They walked on in silence.

# ▲ Chapter Ten ▲

Tekakwitha continued her story after a while. "I could not marry that young man, or in fact, any man. I do not want to marry anyone at all. I want to give my life to Jesus Christ fully."

"You mean, like becoming a Sister or something?" Katie asked. She knew that Sister Margaret, a teacher at her school, was not married. She lived in a big house with other Sisters.

Tekakwitha nodded her head. "Because of this, my family is very angry," she said. "Most of the people of my tribe hate me. They tell false stories about me. They think I am lazy. Their words are as sharp as the rocks along this path," Tekakwitha said. "But even with all of this, my life is filled with hope in God."

Katie could tell that even though she said she was hopeful, Tekakwitha was very sad.

"So the priest came to you?" Katie prompted her, wanting to hear the rest of the story. Maybe it would lead somehow to an explanation of how she'd come to be in this place.

"Father de Lamberville came," Tekakwitha continued. "He asked how he could help me. Even though I was very afraid, I decided to tell him. I wanted to come to know the One True God as my mother had. I wanted to become a Catholic."

"That's awesome!" Katie responded enthusiastically. "I love being Catholic! But why was that so scary for you?"

"As I told you, my uncle hates the Blackrobes and all Christians. My uncle believes that if you follow Jesus, you turn your back on our Mohawk people."

"But you asked Father de Lamberville anyway?" Katie prodded, amazed by Tekakwitha's bravery.

"I did," Tekakwitha responded. Katie saw her smile for the first time since they had met. "Now, I come to the chapel every day. As angry as it made him, my uncle gave his permission."

"What made your uncle change his mind?" Katie asked.

"He wanted to honor the agreement, a treaty that had been made between our people and the Blackrobes," Tekakwitha explained. "I do all of my work. But I also come very early in the morning each day and every evening to the chapel to pray and to study. And I come every Sunday to pray the Mass. I am studying and learning constantly.

I am preparing for a very special day that will come soon."

"Oh, I love Sundays, too," Katie shared happily. "Patrick—he's my twin brother—is always running late. And Hoa Hong, my baby sister, is crawling all over the place. But Sunday is still my favorite day of the week!"

When Katie mentioned her family, Tekakwitha stopped in the middle of the path. She looked at Katie, noticing her pink backpack and Rosie, who was still in Katie's hand.

"I must ask you, young one, how did you come to be in this place? Your clothing is very strange. And you carry a bag on your shoulders. This small horse, does it have special meaning?" asked Tekakwitha, pointing at Rosie. "You appeared so suddenly, I assumed you were sent by God."

"Oh, Tekakwitha," Katie answered quickly. "I honestly don't know how I am here! One moment,

I was praying in our chapel at St. Anne's. Then the bells began to chime...and suddenly I am here! Where exactly are we?"

"Why, this is our village, of course. You are in Caughnawaga, in New York. Our colony used to be called New Netherland," Tekakwitha explained. Somehow, she knew that Katie was very far from home.

"New Netherland?" Katie asked. "But, wait... what year is this?"

"What year?" Tekakwitha said, looking at Katie. She thought this was a very strange question to ask. "This is the year 1675."

Katie exclaimed, "1675!" "Patrick was right!" Her heart began to race. Not only was she lost. Katie was lost in time! For the first time since she had arrived in the longhouse, Katie began to cry.

# ▲ Chapter Eleven ▲

"Calm yourself, young one," Tekakwitha said kindly. "We will find your people. You are safe here. Do not be afraid!" She came closer to Katie, using the red blanket around her shoulders to wipe Katie's tears.

Katie cried for a few more minutes. Tekakwitha stood quietly, looking at the girl's face. "You have a very beautiful spirit, young one," she said softly.

"Beautiful?" Katie said, laughing through her tears. "Erin is beautiful! Lily is beautiful! I'm too tall. I'm the only girl in class with red hair!

And my freckles? I hate them. I am definitely not beautiful..."

"But you are, young one!" Tekakwitha exclaimed. "You are God's beautiful creation! I know it is not a comfort when you are missing your family, but I have never seen hair such as yours. Your hair is the color of a fiery sunset. The spots on your face? Those are God's kisses. And you are tall and strong!"

Katie looked at Tekakwitha. She saw the deep scars in her skin, where the smallpox sores had been. She swallowed her tears and smiled. "Thank you. You are beautiful, too!"

"You are precious, young one!" Tekakwitha grinned. "My beauty comes from loving Christ. God made me as I am, to know and serve him. I am beautiful inside, as you are, because I am loved by God."

Forgetting her fear for a moment, Katie hugged Tekakwitha gently. Then Tekakwitha took the girl's hands. She looked at Rosie and smiled. "I love horses, too," Tekakwitha laughed. "Now, let us go!"

Katie and Tekakwitha continued their walk toward the chapel. Katie looked again at the woman walking next to her. In many ways, Tekakwitha was an outcast, a loner. She was certainly different, and that made her the target of jokes and cruelty. But Tekakwitha was happy and peaceful, too.

Katie thought about Lily. In some ways, this strange young woman beside her reminded her of the new girl. Katie didn't know why. But she did know that hearing of Tekakwitha's challenges left her own heart hurting for the way she had treated Lily.

"You are a great blessing, young one," Tekakwitha said with a smile.

"I *am* blessed!" Katie replied. "And, please, call me Katie. Now let's get to the chapel. I was going to ask Father de Lamberville to borrow his cell phone. But I guess that's not going to happen! But maybe he will know how to help me get home!"

# ▲ Chapter Twelve ▲

Tekakwitha and Katie walked up to another wooden building. It looked just like Tekakwitha's longhouse, only smaller. Tekakwitha smiled. "Welcome to St. Peter's! Let us go inside and visit with Father de Lamberville."

"*This* is the chapel?" Katie asked, confused at the building's simplicity. "But it looks just like another wooden cabin. You pray here?"

"Oh, my friend, this is a place of great worship," Tekakwitha said. "It may look very simple. But this is a place of learning and of prayer. Honestly, I feel as though this is my true home. *Come!*"

Within a few moments of entering the simple chapel, the two were greeted by a friendly man. Before them, stood Father de Lamberville, a Jesuit priest—a member of a religious order called the Society of Jesus. Father was indeed wearing a long black gown. Katie remembered Father Miguel calling it a "cassock" when he had come to class to teach them about the vestments, or clothes, that priests wear.

"Hello, Father," Tekakwitha said with great affection. "I have brought a new friend, Katie. She is new to Caughnawaga. She would like to ask you for your help."

"Ah, *bienvenue*, Katie," Father de Lamberville greeted her. "You are welcome here in St. Peter's!"

"Thank you, Father," Katie responded. Again, she thought about how kindly she had been received here. She was a stranger who had arrived out of nowhere. Then she thought of how unkind

she and her friends had been to Lily. When Lily first came to St. Anne's, no one had welcomed her! This memory made Katie feel sad.

Looking around her, Katie saw some things that looked familiar to her. They were simple versions of the same things in her own church. Katie could easily spot a few beautiful paintings that told familiar Bible stories, and at the front and center of the chapel was a large wooden altar. Somehow, even though she felt so very far from home, these simple things calmed her nerves.

"How may I be of help to you, Katie?" Father de Lamberville asked.

"Well, Father, I am lost. I need to get home to my parents as soon as possible," Katie responded. She decided not to mention the bells chiming, or the fact that she had traveled in time. That sounded too crazy. "I know that they must be very worried about me."

"Lost?" Father de Lamberville asked, looking at Katie's strange clothing and her backpack. Even though he had traveled a lot, he had never seen a young girl dressed like Katie. "I have a brother priest who will be going to the city soon. I am sure he would be happy to take you to your family. He will not be here for a few days. But you are welcome to remain here with us for as long as you would like. You see, we are preparing for a special celebration!"

As he said this, Father de Lamberville looked toward Tekakwitha with a great smile.

"A celebration?" asked Katie. She was never one to miss a party!

"Yes, a beautiful celebration!" he answered. "Tomorrow, as you know, is Easter Sunday. Our Tekakwitha has studied and prepared and prayed for many months. Tomorrow, she will be baptized."

"Easter? Baptized?" Katie asked with both happiness and surprise. Katie could remember two recent and very special baptisms. The first had happened at last year's Easter Vigil when her own dad had been baptized. That same night, he had received his first Holy Communion and had been confirmed into the Catholic faith.

And then, of course, how could she forget precious Hoa Hong's baptism? In her mind, it was hard to disconnect that day with Patrick's frog jumping into the baptismal font. Even with the frog incident, both days were joyful.

*But how could tomorrow be Easter? Then again, how could this be 1675? Katie thought again of Patrick's story, and the bells chiming, and the floor rumbling, and that cold wind...*

*Patrick must be right,* Katie thought to herself. And as impossible as it all seemed, Katie realized that if Patrick was right about his time travel, then she was right about hers. More importantly, it meant that God was in control of this whole crazy situation. She would definitely get back home, just like Patrick had. Katie just wasn't sure when.

Katie took a deep breath and, despite how crazy it all seemed, she decided to *trust*. God had gotten Patrick out of Ireland, so he would get her out of here, too. She just had to watch, wait, and pray. She decided to relax and make the most of

this time.

"How wonderful, Tekakwitha!" Katie smiled, turning to the young woman. "You must be very excited."

"I am so greatly happy," Tekakwitha said. "I have studied and prayed for this day for a very long time."

"Tekakwitha is very humble," Father de Lamberville responded. "Her faith and humility are clear to all of the Christians around her. She is a special young woman. All of them have only good things to say about her. Will you join us tomorrow as Tekakwitha is baptized?"

"Well," Katie replied with uncertainty. "I need to figure out a way to get back to my family as soon as possible. But if I am still here tomorrow, I'd love to celebrate with you!"

Even though she wanted to get home, Katie hoped that she would be around one more day to see Tekakwitha be baptized. Then she would figure out how to get back home!

# ▲ Chapter Thirteen ▲

As they walked away from the chapel, Katie found herself both frightened and fascinated. It was getting dark. Katie realized that she would have to spend the night at the longhouse with Tekakwitha, the chief, and his family.

"Can we stop here and pray together?" Katie asked Tekakwitha. She knew that it wouldn't be safe for her new friend to pray in front of her uncle.

Together, the two of them knelt near a large tree in the woods outside the longhouse. In the moonlight, they prayed out loud and in silence.

Katie was amazed that even though Tekakwitha had not yet been baptized, she was such a beautiful young woman.

And by *beautiful*, Katie didn't mean that she was very pretty to look at. Instead, it was like there was a light around Tekakwitha. Katie thought about that light—*whatever it was*—and she wanted to be more like Tekakwitha.

After they had prayed, they joined Tekakwitha's family in the longhouse. The women worked together to prepare dinner. The food was simple and served in bowls. Katie felt afraid to eat it at first. But she was so hungry that she soon joined in. The time passed quickly.

Tekakwitha's heart was filled with kindness. As they cooked and ate, Katie watched how the members of Tekakwitha's own family treated her very unkindly. But instead of yelling back at them, Tekakwitha was quiet and loving.

Watching Tekakwitha, Katie thought about the times she had argued with Patrick or not listened to her parents. She thought of Lily and her friends Erin and Maria. *Why couldn't I have been nicer?* she asked herself.

After dinner, Tekakwitha made a small sleeping area on the floor for Katie. She covered her with a woven blanket to make sure Katie was warm. As she tucked Katie into bed, Tekakwitha whispered a prayer for Katie's family. Then she prayed for her own family and for the members of her tribe. She prayed that Katie would find her way home safely. Tekakwitha prayed that her family would come to know Jesus, too.

Snuggling under the warm blanket with Rosie, Katie whispered, "Please, God! Amen!"

# ▲ Chapter Fourteen ▲

The next morning, the sun rose early. Tekakwitha woke Katie. It was so cold inside the longhouse that Katie shivered. She was wearing jeans and a hoodie, but was still freezing.

Tekakwitha stood over her holding a warm blue woolen blanket, just like the red one she wore to cover her face. She draped the blanket around Katie's shoulders saying, "It is time to go to the chapel!"

"Easter Sunday!" thought Katie to herself. "I wonder if it's Easter back at home..." Katie decided that she would go to Mass with Tekakwitha and then focus on how she could get back home. *Maybe somehow being at the chapel would help...*

As soon as Tekakwitha had helped with the morning chores, it was time to go to church. As they walked towards the chapel longhouse, Tekakwitha stopped. She bent down to the ground and picked up two sticks. Working quickly in the cold morning air, Tekakwitha made the sticks into a small cross. She handed the wooden cross to Katie.

"It's beautiful!" Katie smiled.

"Keep it," Tekakwitha said quietly. "I have many of these. I make them and spread them around the paths in this forest. And I carve small crosses into the trees to remind myself that Jesus is always with me, even when I feel sad or afraid."

"Thank you." Katie slipped the small cross into her pocket. The air around her was cold. The ground was covered with a light frost. But

Katie felt warm with her hood pulled over her head and the blue blanket around her shoulders. It was long enough to almost cover her jeans, but her tennis shoes still showed. Normally for Easter, Katie wore a beautiful dress. *Not this year*, she thought to herself...

Katie was surprised that Tekakwitha's family did not seem to be doing anything at all to celebrate her special day. In fact, they had all seemed angry at breakfast that Tekakwitha was going to church, and they weren't afraid to tell her that.

But when Tekakwitha and Katie arrived at the chapel longhouse, Katie saw that it was overflowing with people. Even the people who were not Christian had come. They were curious to see what would happen! The chapel was decorated with animal pelts, feathers, ribbons, wildflowers, and pine branches.

It was a beautiful Easter morning! Katie thought about how different it was from the way her family celebrated at St. Anne's and at home on Easter Sunday. Tekakwitha changed into a simple white dress that Father de Lamberville gave her. She came forward with two other young women.

Katie watched Tekakwitha kneel down at the front of the chapel. She heard Tekakwitha make a profession of her faith, declaring that she believed in God and in the Church.

Catherine of Siena "Kateri"

Tekakwitha prayed the Apostles' Creed out loud. Katie smiled as she remembered learning the Creed and the Our Father at St. Anne's. The words reminded her of home and of her family.

"I can't wait to get home!" Katie whispered to Rosie. "Wait until Patrick hears about this!"

Then Father de Lamberville recited the words of baptism. He poured water over Tekakwitha's head. He gave her a new name "Catherine of Siena," after a beautiful young saint who had given herself fully to Jesus Christ. Katie smiled. *I was named after St. Catherine!* she thought.

After the Easter Mass, Katie was filled with joy. She rushed to Tekakwitha with a big smile on her face. "Congratulations, my new sister in Christ!" she said, hugging Tekakwitha as if she had known her forever. "I am so happy that I was here today with you, Tekakwitha!"

"Please," the young woman said with a smile, "Call me by my new name, *Kateri*."

"Kateri?" Katie asked out loud. *"Tekakwitha?"*

Suddenly, behind her she heard a familiar sound. Katie turned and saw Father de Lamberville standing at the door. He had a big smile on his face and a small silver bell in his hand.

Below her feet, Katie felt the ground rumble. The chiming of the small bell grew stronger and a cold wind rushed around her.

And suddenly everything became a blur.

# ▲ Chapter Fifteen ▲

"Wake up!" Katie heard a whispered voice saying urgently in the dark.

Katie sat up, startled that she was again beginning another day so far away from home. As her eyes adjusted to the dim lighting in the longhouse, she felt like she had been asleep for a very long time. *But wait,* Katie thought. *I was just at the chapel...*

As she started to wake up, Katie remembered Father's silver bell chiming and the ground rumbling and that cold rushing wind. She looked around herself, wondering if she was back at St. Anne's.

Almost immediately, Katie realized that she wasn't. But something was different...she just wasn't sure what.

In front of Katie was a young woman who looked a lot like her friend Tekakwitha telling her again, "Hurry up!" Katie remembered that she was supposed to call her "Kateri" now. But this Kateri looked older. And she looked much more serious!

It was all so confusing. Katie began to feel tears and panic well up inside of her. *How will I ever get home?*

"We must go," Kateri whispered, looking around her. *"Now!"*

"Go where?" Katie asked, sitting up. "Did you figure out a way to get me home?"

"Not yet. We are leaving now to go to the Mission at Sault St. Louis," Kateri whispered. For the past few years since my baptism, my life here has become more and more difficult. It is time to get away!"

"*The past few years?*" Katie whispered back, reaching for her backpack and checking to see that Rosie was still clipped on top of it. "Where are we? I mean, *when* are we?"

Then Katie's mind flashed back to Easter. *Wasn't that just yesterday?* she asked herself.

*But the priest, and the bell, and the rumbling, and the wind...* Katie thought.

She started to put some of the pieces together in her mind. "Patrick told me about the bells chiming," Katie whispered to Rosie. "*We must have moved forward in time...but not far enough to get home!*"

As she finished her packing, Kateri didn't seem to hear Katie's questions. She went on, telling Katie her story as she grabbed a bit of food. She put the food and a few pieces of paper into a small basket while she talked.

"My family members here do not understand my love for God," Kateri explained sadly. "Since Sunday is the Lord's Day and I spend that day in prayer and not working, they refuse to feed me. The people in this village throw rocks at me and call me names."

"They throw rocks at you?" Katie asked. "Just because you want to go to church?"

"I am willing to offer this as a sacrifice for God, out of love for him," Kateri tried to explain. "But now, my older sister and her husband have sent for me. They are new Christians, and they went away to live at the Mission. They made a plan for me to escape and live there! Since my uncle is away on a trading mission, I will go there today before he can return and refuse to let me leave."

"But what about me?" Katie said, panicking. "What will happen? How will I ever get home?"

"Don't worry, Katie!" Kateri reassured her with a hug. "Father de Lamberville has written letters for me to introduce me to the Blackrobes at the St. Francis Xavier Mission. Father told them that I am a Christian. You will come with me. The Blackrobes there will surely welcome both of us. They will take care of us."

Even though she could tell by Kateri's frightened expression that this would be a dangerous trip, Katie knew that she had no choice. She needed to go along with Kateri. Maybe at the Mission, she would finally figure out how to get back to St. Anne's.

# ▲ Chapter Sixteen ▲

The two of them left immediately with nothing but the clothes on their backs, Katie's backpack with Rosie, and a small basket that Kateri carried. Inside the basket were the letters from Father de Lamberville and some food. Father had told Kateri to place all of her trust in God. Katie knew that she too had to trust that everything would eventually work out.

Over the next six days, Katie and Kateri went on a long, dangerous canoe trip. They paddled and hiked and crossed rivers and lakes. Katie lost all track of time, but she began to give up her

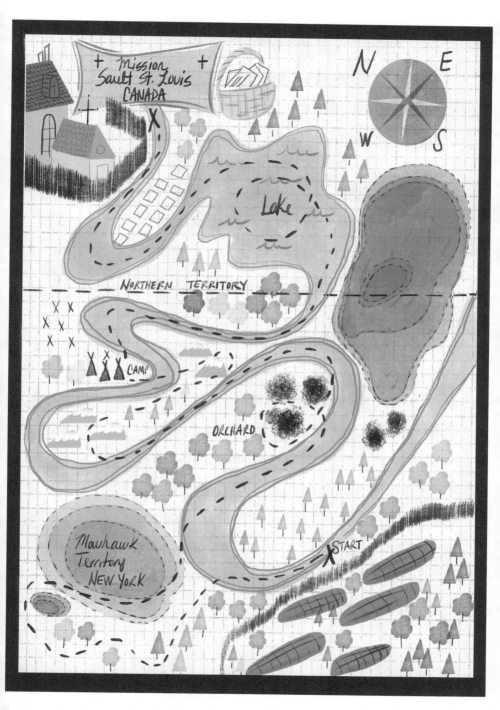

fear that she would never get home. Along with Kateri and the two other men who were their protectors and guides, Katie prayed constantly.

This place was so different from her home. When they needed to eat, the guides would catch a fish or Kateri would gather berries along the side of the riverbank. At night, they camped under the stars. To Katie, the trip began to feel like an adventure.

*"Wait until Patrick hears about this,"* Katie thought at least once a day.

Finally, the small band of travelers arrived at the Mission. Kateri's adoptive sister welcomed her. In the Mission there were three priests, all with long French names. They were all Blackrobes, too!

As they arrived to welcome the new Christians to their Mission, Kateri gave one of the priests, Father Cholenec, the letters from Father de

Lamberville. Father Cholenec read the words his brother priest had written about young Kateri.

*It is a treasure which we are giving you, as you will soon realize. Guard it well...*

Katie watched Kateri settle into a routine. For the first time ever, her friend was free to pray openly without being afraid. Kateri and Katie prayed the rosary every day. And best of all, Kateri and Katie went to Mass every Sunday together. Kateri was no longer an outcast here in the Mission. In this place, no one teased her about the scars on her face or her bad eyesight.

For the first time, she was able to teach others about her faith. Kateri became a teacher for the children of the Mission. Katie helped teach, too, creating simple crafts for the younger children and teaching them their prayers.

The priests at the Mission soon noticed that Kateri was truly ready to receive the Eucharist. The day she had waited for would soon come!

Katie learned to love life at the Mission. It wasn't easy—there were chores to be done. The weather was cold. She often felt hungry. Even the most basic things like cooking and washing clothes took hours. She also missed her family so much that it hurt.

But she loved the way that Mission life seemed to revolve around prayer. She too loved God, loved going to church and reading the Bible.

But as much as Katie was getting used to Mission life, she never stopped trying to figure out how to get home. She prayed every day, but it quickly became clear that something important was missing. Patrick had been able to travel in time too, and he had come home safely. Katie felt sure that she would get home someday. But she was having a very hard time waiting to see her family.

Watching Kateri pray made Katie realize how much she had taken her own faith for granted. At home, Katie could go to church any time she wanted. She had parents who loved her and prayed with her all the time. She could receive Holy Communion every day of the week if she wanted!

As she spent time at the Mission, Katie thought a lot about Lily. When she and Kateri had come here, they were welcomed and made many new friends. But when Lily had come to St. Anne's, no one had welcomed her. In fact, Katie and her friends had been extra mean to Lily. Katie promised herself that when she got back to St. Anne's, she would go out of her way to be nice to Lily.

Kateri began another time of prayer and study. She was preparing for her first Holy Communion. Katie remembered the day that she and Patrick had received their first Communion a few years ago. The twins had enjoyed a special Mass with all of their classmates. Mom and Dad had hosted a party in the backyard that Saturday in May. But Kateri's special day wouldn't be in May. The priests planned for Kateri to make her first Holy Communion at Mass on Christmas!

Just thinking about that made Katie smile. But it also made her homesick. The longer she spent at the Mission, the more Katie wondered if she would ever find a way to get back home.

Kateri kept Katie's secret safe. She didn't know how Katie had come to be there. But Kateri trusted in God, and she constantly told Katie to trust, too. As the weather grew colder, Katie wrapped herself in blankets and animal pelts.

She began to look more and more like the girls of the Mission.

At the end of every day, Katie was exhausted, but also happy. Even though she wanted to go home, Katie was amazed by the things she saw and learned. She had read about this time in history class. But being here was like seeing her history book come to life!

Katie slept next to Kateri, holding her little pink horse, Rosie. Saying her prayers and holding Rosie reminded Katie that God was with her in this place. She had a funny feeling that she would be home soon. She missed her family more with every day that went by.

"God, I know you are teaching me many lessons here," Katie prayed. "Thank you for this adventure, whatever it is! Please keep my family safe. Please teach me to love everyone. And please bring me home to St. Anne's soon!"

# ▲ Chapter Seventeen ▲

Soon, it was the day for Kateri's First Communion: Christmas Day!

As she entered the church with Kateri, Katie saw that it had been decorated especially for Christmas. She smiled at the sight of the simple nativity set and at little baby Jesus in the manger. She was so very far from home, and yet in this place she felt safe—almost like she was back at St. Anne's. She prayed for her family, who were surely missing her, hoping that they knew that she was safe and thinking of them.

As Christmas Mass was celebrated, Katie anticipated the moment she knew Kateri had been waiting for so many years. The people in the church sang quietly as Kateri went forward to the Communion rail at the front of the church and knelt down.

Watching Kateri, Katie realized that this is what she wanted to feel like from now on when she went to receive Communion. Sure, she had been excited when she and Patrick had made their First Communions. But Katie realized that she should feel that same joy every Sunday, every time she received Jesus in the Eucharist.

Kateri received the Body of Christ for the very first time with tears of joy streaming down her face.

Nearby, Katie kneeled and closed her eyes in quiet prayer. She thanked God for loving her

so much that he would send his very own Son, Jesus, to save her. Katie smiled, thinking about how much she had learned from Kateri. She had learned to love God, but also to love herself more, too. Somehow Kateri had taught her that it didn't matter if her hair or clothes weren't perfect. Who she was on the inside and what she did to share God's love with others around her was far more important.

After Communion, a choir of children from the Mission began to sing. As they sang, Kateri stood with them, shaking a silver bell in time with the words of the Christmas carol. Katie felt a rush of warmth and peace fill her whole body as she listened to the song.

As Kateri's small silver bell chimed in her ears, Katie heard a sound in the distance—a familiar sound, a sound that was calling her home.

Katie felt the ground of the chapel begin to rumble.

A strong rush of cold wind blew the doors of the chapel wide open.

And suddenly, everything became a blur.

# ▲ Chapter Eighteen ▲

*Clang, clang, clang...*

As the loud Angelus bells of St. Anne's chimed, Katie opened her eyes.

She was kneeling in the front pew of the St. Anne's Adoration Chapel. Around her, the candles flickered and there was no sound but the ringing of the bells and the nearby sound of a vacuum.

Katie grabbed her backpack, which was mysteriously right next to her again, and looked for Rosie. Seeing the horse made her laugh out loud. "We're home!"

Standing up, Katie remembered to genuflect, dropping down to one knee before hurrying out of the chapel.

"Dad, Patrick!" Katie yelled, running from the front of the church towards the back pews where they were organizing the hymnals. "I'm *home!*"

She was too excited to see the shocked look on her dad's face or the smile on her brother's.

"I'm so sorry! I can't believe I was gone for so long," Katie shouted, forgetting to use her inside church voice. "I missed Easter, but at least I am back to have Christmas dinner with you! How is Hoa Hong? She must be almost walking by now. Oh, Patrick, you should have seen it—the forest was amazing, and..."

"Slow down, Katie," Dad whispered, reminding her that she'd been talking too loudly inside the church. "What is this about Christmas?"

"*Ummm,*" Patrick started with a laugh, winking

at Katie, "Haven't you heard about our big 'Christmas in May' project at school? It's gonna be great..."

Patrick saw Father Miguel quietly walking towards the Adoration Chapel.

"In May?" Katie asked in confusion. "But Kateri's first Communion, and..."

"Come on, Katie," Patrick interrupted. "I think Father Miguel needs us in the Adoration Chapel."

Leading his sister by the arm down the center aisle, Patrick glanced towards Father Miguel's confessional.

"You weren't, by any chance, cleaning the confessionals this morning, were you?" Patrick asked. "I think I finally know what's going on here..."

"The confessionals? What? No!" Katie growled back at him. "I was in the chapel saying a prayer. And then all of a sudden..."

She paused, looking around. Everything looked exactly the same as it had before she'd left. But it felt like many months had passed.

Katie looked down in shock at her jeans and tennis shoes. She was surprised to see them clean instead of caked with mud. Even Rosie was bright pink and clean again.

"I'm confused," Katie whispered, stopping Patrick.

"Katie, where did you go? What was it like? Patrick asked in a quiet but excited voice. "When was it? Who did you meet?"

"Patrick, Katie, *mis mellizos*, my twins," Father Miguel spoke to them from the front pew of the Adoration Chapel where he was kneeling. Standing, the priest genuflected reverently, making the Sign of the Cross. He walked to where the twins were standing. Then he silently led them out of the chapel.

"Come sit down with me for a few minutes." He led them towards the pew closest to his confessional.

Patrick was disappointed. He just wanted to talk to Katie alone and find out all about her adventure. Katie seemed anxious to tell their priest all about her journey. Patrick wasn't sure that was a great idea.

"I'm so glad to see you, Father Miguel," Katie began as she stepped into the pew. "There were these priests in the forest, the Blackrobes. Do you know any of them?"

"The Blackrobes?" Patrick giggled. "Is that the name of your new basketball team, Father Miguel?" Katie looked at her brother, then shook her head, finally understanding.

"Hey, not a bad idea, Patrick," Father Miguel chuckled. "Let's talk later, Katie..."

"Great idea, Father Miguel," Patrick agreed. Katie caught his eye and smiled, silently agreeing not to tell Father Miguel until she'd spoken to Patrick.

"I'm so glad you're both here today," Father Miguel continued. "I have a special mission for you..."

"*A mission?*" the twins asked at the same time.

# ▲ Chapter Nineteen ▲

At that moment, the door to Father Miguel's confessional slid open and out came Lily, dust rag in hand. "All done, Padre, " she said with a shy smile. Patrick and Katie could smell the lemon-scented cleaning spray in the air.

"Thanks, Lily!" Father Miguel said. "Twins, here is your special mission," he continued, smiling toward Lily.

"Lily?" Katie asked, suddenly feeling a rush of sorrow. She immediately remembered how mean she'd been to the new girl for the past few weeks.

"Do you want to tell them, Lily?" Father Miguel asked.

"Father, do you mind if I talk with Lily for a minute first?" Katie asked. Father Miguel nodded, and Katie moved away from Patrick and the priest.

"Lily," Katie said when Lily followed her. "I'm really sorry I have been so mean to you."

Tears filled Lily's eyes and she blinked them away. "It's OK, Katie..."

"No, Lily," Katie said. "It's not OK! I was afraid that if I was nice to you, I would lose my friends. You're so pretty and sweet." Lily blushed as Katie continued. "I was jealous. I'm sorry."

Lily smiled at her. "I forgive you!" They exchanged a hug. "Let's go back to Father Miguel. I want you to hear my news."

"Father, I'm ready to tell the twins my news now!" Lily said as they came back to the priest and Patrick. "You know I'm new here to St. Anne's. The truth is, I'm new to the Church, too!" Lily said in an excited voice. "When I was younger, I was baptized at my dad's church. He wasn't Catholic, but he and my mom wanted me to know Jesus. I have an old picture from that day, with the three of us. It's a special picture to me, now that Dad's gone..."

The twins watched as Lily braced herself from the wave of sadness that started to rush over her.

"I'd like to see that photo some day," Katie said encouragingly.

"Well, that was a long time ago," Lily continued, "and a lot has happened since then. You know my mom and I came here to live with my grandparents, and they are members of St. Anne's. I've been coming to Mass with Nana and Gramps. And now, Father Miguel and Mrs. Ray think that maybe I am almost ready to receive the Eucharist!"

The twins looked at their priest for his reaction.

"It's true, kids," Father Miguel smiled. "Lily has a true love for Jesus. She wants to make her First Communion and I would love for her to do that during Mass on Pentecost. But she needs to have some extra study and preparation..."

"... and that's where we come in!" Katie said brightly. "We would love to help you prepare for your First Communion, Lily!"

"Sure, Lily," Patrick echoed shyly.

"Oh, that would be so great!" Lily's smile was bright enough to light up all of St. Anne's.

# ▲ Chapter Twenty ▲

*Clang, clang, clang...*

*Clang, clang, clang...*

The sound of Miss Elizabeth's triangle rang out as Katie and Lily laughed together. They were standing side by side at Reinhard's Stables on another Friday afternoon in their helmets and boots.

"Are you sure you don't want to ride Belle today, Katie?" Lily asked as they groomed their horses.

"You go ahead," Katie said. "I'm actually starting to like Peerybingle! He keeps me on my toes with that attitude of his. Riding him is always an adventure!"

As they finished their preparations and mounted their horses for the lesson, Lily gave Katie a genuine smile.

"You're so awesome, Katie," she said.

Katie swallowed the lump that was forming in the back of her throat, trying to avoid apologizing yet again for how mean she had been when Lily had first come to school. The girls had found a way to put that behind them, and Lily had told Katie that she didn't need to keep apologizing.

"We *both* are, aren't we?" Katie responded, laughing.

These past few weeks, praying, reading, studying, and just hanging out with Lily had been a gift for Katie. While she saw Lily growing in her knowledge of the Catholic faith and her love for Jesus, Katie felt herself growing, too.

For so long, Katie had felt as if everyone else was *better* than her. The girls—even her best friends—were cuter, had nicer clothes and better hair, and were more into the popular stuff than she was. Katie had always felt so out of it, like everyone else knew a secret that she could never quite figure out. She had wanted to be more like Erin or Maria. But lately, she was learning to be happy with being herself.

Somehow, spending time with Lily had helped Katie to realize that she'd known the answer to that secret all along. Katie remembered back to that day at St. Anne's when she had gone on what Patrick was now calling her "chime traveler adventure."

Since that day, Katie had been reading all about the saint she simply liked to call "Kateri." When Katie thought about Lily, she saw that her new friend was just like the young Native American,

St. Kateri Tekakwitha. Lily, just like Tekakwitha, had a hunger to know God, to be a part of the Church, and to receive Jesus in the Eucharist.

St. Kateri's face may have been scarred, but her heart and soul were pure and beautiful. Katie knew now that beauty was more than what you saw on the outside of a person. True beauty came from inside, from love. Ever since her adventure with Kateri, Katie had felt her own love for Jesus growing. She was learning to love herself just as God loved her!

And as this happened, the pieces of herself that had never been good enough were starting to feel just right. Katie realized that Dad was right when he said, "God doesn't make junk!"

"Come on, Lily," Katie said. "Let's ride!

# ▲ Chapter Twenty-One ▲

Two days later, the bells of St. Anne's rang out, calling the families to Mass on Pentecost Sunday. The chimes could be heard from miles away.

Patrick was up on the altar serving. Katie knelt in the pew with her family, right behind Lily, her mom and her grandparents. Katie smiled at Lily in her beautiful white dress and simple white veil she wore over her hair.

Before the opening prayer, Fr. Miguel welcomed them and said loudly, "Happy Birthday!"

"Happy Birthday," the families of St. Anne's responded joyfully. Father Miguel reminded them that Pentecost was the "birthday of the Church." The very first Pentecost happened fifty days after Jesus was resurrected. The Holy Spirit came down upon the disciples that day. The Spirit made them brave enough to go out and tell others about Jesus. Father Miguel taught them that Pentecost was really the start of the Catholic Church, the Church's "birthday." Pentecost was a perfect day for Lily's first Communion.

Katie smiled at her little sister Hoa Hong, balanced on Mom's hip. Then she looked up at the altar and stuck her tongue out at Patrick. This made her laugh because when Patrick was altar serving, he couldn't do anything about her teasing! Looking around, Katie sent up a silent prayer of thanksgiving for this big family—her faith family at St. Anne's. It was really a special "birthday" for all of them!

When the time for Communion came, Father Miguel invited Lily and her family to come forward first. Lily bowed deeply and raised her hands together toward Father Miguel, making a "throne" to receive Jesus in the Eucharist. When Father Miguel held the consecrated Host high in front of her with the words, "The Body of Christ," Lily's response could be heard throughout the entire church.

"Amen!"

That Pentecost Sunday, as each of the parishioners of St. Anne's came forward to receive Jesus, truly present in Holy Communion, that same loud, clear, "Amen!" rang out over and over again.

Katie knelt in the pew after receiving Communion, giving thanks for her family and her special new friend, Lily.

"Thank you, Jesus. I love you, Jesus!" she whispered.

Mr. Sarkisian and the choir began to sing a special song, and above her Katie heard the choir bells play along with the singing:

*"Come Holy Ghost, creator blessed,*
*and in our hearts take up thy rest..."*

Katie thought of St. Kateri Tekakwitha and the joy that the saint had modeled in coming to know Jesus Christ. Katie realized now more than ever that her faith, her Church, and her family were all amazing gifts from God.

*"Chime travelers..."* Katie smiled to herself as the loud bells began to ring.

*Clang, clang, clang...*

As the bells of St. Anne's chimed outside, Katie slipped her hand into the pocket of her skirt to grab her rosary.

Startled, Katie looked down at her hand, which held the beads Lily had given her as a thank-you gift...

...and, woven together from two small sticks, one simple wooden cross.

# ▲ The Real St. Kateri Tekakwitha ▲

Much of what we know about the life of St. Kateri Tekakwitha comes from biographies that were written by the Jesuit priests, members of the religious order of the Society of Jesus, who helped the saint prepare to receive the sacraments of baptism and First Communion.

Tekakwitha was born in 1656 in Osserneon (now called Auriesville) in what is now the state of New York. Her mother, a Christian Algonquin, was captured by the Iroquois and later married Tekakwitha's father, a Mohawk chief who was not a Christian.

When Tekakwitha was four years old, her tribe suffered from a terrible smallpox outbreak. The illness killed Tekakwitha's parents and younger brother. She was adopted by her uncle and his family and lived with them as their daughter. As a result of her smallpox, Tekakwitha (whose name means "One who places things in order") suffered from scars that covered her face and greatly weakened eyesight. Because the bright light hurt her eyes, she often did her work indoors and covered her head and eyes with a blanket when she went outdoors.

Despite the protests of her family, Father Jacques de Lamberville baptized Tekakwitha on Easter Sunday in 1676, naming her Catherine, rendered "Kateri" in her language, after St. Catherine of Siena. In July of 1677, Kateri escaped from her village and traveled over two hundred miles to the Catholic mission of St. Francis Xavier at Sault St. Louis, near Montreal in Canada.

At the mission, Kateri was known for her great faithfulness. She received special instructions in the faith and received her First Holy Communion on Christmas Day, 1677. She continued to live a life of great service, vowing not to marry and living in community with other religious women.

Kateri's health began to suffer greatly and she died at the age of twenty-four on April 17, 1680. The priests who served in her community and knew her well wrote of her tremendous love for Jesus and the Church.

Kateri Tekakwitha was proclaimed a saint on October 21, 2012, by Pope Benedict XVI, after it was determined that she had interceded in the miraculous healing of a five-year-old with a life-threatening disease.

St. Kateri Tekakwitha is a patroness for the environment and for those who have lost a parent. You can learn more about this special saint at http://www.katerishrine.com or http://www.tekakwitha.info.

# ▲ A Prayer in Honor of
# St. Kateri Tekakwitha ▲

*Collect of the Mass in honor of St. Kateri Tekakwitha from the Roman Missal:*

Lord God, you called the virgin St. Kateri Tekakwitha, to shine among the American Indian people as an example of innocence of life. Through her intercession, may all peoples of every tribe, tongue and nation, having been gathered into Your Church, proclaim your greatness in one song of praise. We ask this through our Lord Jesus Christ, Your Son, Who lives and reigns with You and the Holy Spirit, one God, forever and ever. Amen.

# ▲ A Prayer Before Communion ▲

Dear Jesus, I pray today to receive you in this Communion with faith that you are truly present in the Eucharist.

I am sorry for my sins.

I come to you in love and belief.

Fill my heart with your grace, and help me to share your love with all the world.

Amen.

# ▲ Discussion Questions ▲

1. In the beginning of this book, we meet Lily, the new girl at St. Anne's. Have you ever been to a new school or welcomed a new student to your classroom? How were you welcomed or what did you do to help the new friend feel welcomed?

2. Katie and Patrick help their mom by taking their little sister, Hoa Hong, out for a walk. What are some ways you help your family?

3. Katie is very mean to Lily, the new girl in school, because she feels insecure about herself. Do you ever feel worried that others will not like you because of your clothes, appearance, or family circumstances?

4. Patrick senses that his twin sister, Katie, is upset and tries to talk with her. Who do

you talk with when you are feeling upset or discouraged?

6.  Katie shares with Tekakwitha that she loves Sundays and going to Mass with her family. How does your family usually spend Sundays?

7.  Tekakwitha is baptized on Easter Sunday and given the new name "Kateri," after St. Catherine of Siena. What do you know about the day of your baptism? Do you have any favorite saints?

8.  Kateri is overjoyed on the day of her First Communion. How do you prepare your heart to receive Jesus in the Eucharist?

9.  Katie and Patrick volunteer to help Lily prepare for her sacrament. Do you have any friends who do not know anything about God? How can you share your faith with them?

# The Chime Travelers Series

## by LISA M. HENDEY

When the bells chime, get ready for adventure and fun as you join Katie and Patrick on their travels back in time to far-distant lands. The mysterious strangers they meet along the way turn out to be saints of old who become close friends who help our young travelers understand their faith a little better. Are you ready for the trip of a lifetime? Be ready when you hear the bells chime.

## Available Now!

### *The Secret of the Shamrock*

Patrick travels to Ireland with a frog named Francis and finds himself in a muddy field full of sheep with personality and a mysterious shepherd. As they race across Ireland in response to a secret call, you will find your own faith in God growing stronger.

ISBN 978-1-61636-847-0 | $5.99

# Further Adventures Are on the Way!

## Follow the fun at facebook.com/chimetravelerkids